D0783729

This book belongs to

_____

Mr Peabody

Billy Little

Mr PEABODY'S Apples

by

MADONNA

art by LOREN LONG

PUFFIN

A CALLAWAY EDITION

Mr Peabody congratulates his Little League team on a great game.

IN THE TOWN OF HAPPVILLE

(which wasn't a very big town), Mr Peabody was congratulating his Little League team on a great game. They had not won, but no one really cared because they'd had such a good time playing.

Mr Peabody was a history teacher at the local school and during the summer, he dedicated every Saturday to organizing baseball games with other schools.

Billy Little (who wasn't a very big boy) was one of Mr Peabody's students. He loved baseball more than anything, and he thought Mr Peabody was the greatest. After each game, Billy would always help to pick up all the bats and balls. And when they were finished, Mr Peabody would smile and say, "Thanks, Billy, good job. I'll see you next Saturday."

Then he would start his walk home along the main street of Happville (which wasn't a very big street) waving hello to everyone he knew, and everyone would wave hello back. Along the way, he always passed Mr Funkadeli's fruit market. Here Mr Peabody would stop and admire Mr Funkadeli's fresh apples. He would pick out the shiniest apple, drop it in his bag and continue on his way.

Across the street, Tommy Tittlebottom watched with curiosity as Mr Peabody walked away with the apple.

"That's strange," Tommy said to himself. "Mr Peabody didn't pay anyone for that apple."

Tommy got on his skateboard and rushed to tell his friends.

Mr Peabody picks the shiniest apple.

Tommy and his friends are amazed at what they see.

The following Saturday, Mr Peabody's team played another game and they lost (as usual), but no one seemed to care because they'd had such a good time playing. Billy picked up the balls and bats, and Mr Peabody set off on his walk home. He waved to everyone he knew and they waved back. Once again, he stopped outside Mr Funkadeli's fruit market, picked up the shiniest apple, dropped it in his bag and continued on his way.

Across the street, Tommy Tittlebottom and his friends watched Mr Peabody and they were amazed at what they saw. Mr Peabody had not paid for his apple. They couldn't wait to tell all of their friends, who told their parents, who told their neighbours, who told their friends, in the town of Happville (which wasn't a very big town).

The Saturday after that, Mr Peabody was standing all alone on the baseball field, wondering where everybody was. Then he saw Billy walking towards him with a sad look on his face.

"Hello, Billy. I am glad you're here, but where is the rest of the team?" asked Mr Peabody.

Billy remained silent.

"What is it, Billy?" he asked again.

Billy didn't look up.

"Everybody thinks you're a thief," he said to the ground.

Mr Peabody looked confused. He took off his hat and scratched his head. "Who says I am a thief, Billy? And what did I steal?" he asked.

"Tommy Tittlebottom and his friends said they saw you take an apple from Mr Funkadeli's fruit market, twice, and they said you didn't pay for them," answered Billy.

"Ahh," said Mr Peabody, putting his hat back on his head. "Let's go and talk to Mr Funkadeli about it, shall we?"

Mr Peabody wonders where everybody is.

"Everybody thinks you are a thief."

Billy and Mr Peabody walked down the main street (which wasn't a very big street) and Mr Peabody waved to all the people he knew, but now some of them did not wave back and some pretended they did not even see him. They finally arrived at Mr Funkadeli's fruit market.

Out popped Mr Funkadeli, who said, "Hey, what are you doing here, Mr Peabody? Why aren't you at the game?"

"There wasn't a game today," said Mr Peabody, "and I was wondering if I could take my apple earlier than usual?"

"Sure, why not?" replied Mr Funkadeli. "You pay for them every Saturday morning when you pick up your milk, so you can take them when you like. You want the big shiny one, Mr Peabody?"

Mr Peabody took his apple, smiled, and offered it to Billy.

"I would like to take the apple, Mr Peabody, but I have to go and find Tommy and explain everything," said Billy.

"When you find him, ask him to come over to my house. I would like to speak to him, too," replied Mr Peabody.

Mr Peabody offers Billy the apple.

A little while later, Billy found Tommy and told him what had happened with the apples. He told Tommy that Mr Peabody wanted to speak to him right away. So off Tommy ran and when he arrived, he rang the doorbell. Mr Peabody came to the door. They looked at each other for a while.

"Oh dear, Mr Peabody," said Tommy, on the doorstep. "I didn't understand. I should not have said what I said, but it looked like you hadn't paid for the apples."

Mr Peabody's eyebrows went up a little and he felt a warm breeze blow across his face. "It doesn't matter what it looked like," he said. "What matters is the truth."

Tommy looked down at his shoes and said, "I am so sorry. What can I do to make things better, now?"

Mr Peabody took a deep breath, looked up at a small cloud that was in the sky and said, "I'll tell you what, Tommy. Meet me at the baseball diamond in one hour and bring a pillow stuffed with feathers."

"OK," said Tommy, who then ran off to his house to get a pillow.

Tommy rings Mr Peabody's doorbell.

An hour later, Tommy met Mr Peabody on the pitcher's mound.

"Hello, Tommy," said Mr Peabody. "Follow me and bring your pillow."

Tommy followed Mr Peabody to the top of the bleachers, wondering what this was all about.

"It's a windy day, isn't it?" asked Mr Peabody when they reached the top. Tommy nodded his head in agreement.

"Here is a pair of scissors," continued Mr Peabody. "Now cut the pillow in half and shake the feathers out."

Tommy looked confused, but did it anyway. He thought it was a small price to pay to gain Mr Peabody's forgiveness. The wind carried the thousands of feathers far and wide.

Tommy meets Mr Peabody at the pitcher's mound.

The wind carries the thousands of feathers far and wide.

"Each feather represents a person in Happville."

Tommy looked relieved and said, "Is that all I have to do to make things better?"

"There is one more thing," said Mr Peabody. "Now you must go and pick up all the feathers."

Tommy frowned.

"I don't think it's possible to pick up all the feathers," Tommy replied.

"It would be just as impossible to undo the damage that you have done by spreading the rumour that I am a thief," said Mr Peabody. "Each feather represents a person in Happville."

There was a long pause as Tommy began to understand what Mr Peabody was saying.

Finally, he said, "I guess I have a lot of work ahead of me."

Mr Peabody smiled and said, "Indeed, you do. Next time, don't be so quick to judge a person. And remember the power of your words."

Then he handed Tommy the shiny red apple and made his way home.

Mr Peabody makes his way home.

The end

Dedicated to teachers everywhere

This book was inspired by a nearly 300-year-old story that was told to me by my Kabbalah teacher. It stayed with me for a long time, and when I began to write books for children, I decided to share the essence of this story in one of them.

It is about the power of words.
And how we must choose them carefully to avoid causing harm to others.

The Baal Shem Tov – "Master of the Good Name" – who was the author of the original story, was also a great teacher. He was born c.1700 in Podolia, a region of the Ukraine, and dedicated his life to teaching and helping others. He believed that practising religion out of habit is a pointless endeavour and advocated, instead, an understanding of why we practise spirituality. Among his many teachings, he stressed the value and importance of love for all people.

I hope that I have done his story justice.

MADONNA

PUFFIN BOOKS

Published by the Penguin Group: London, New York, Australia,
Canada, India, New Zealand and South Africa
Penguin Books Ltd, Registered Offices: 80 Strand, London WC2R oRL, England

www.penguin.com

First published in Great Britain in Puffin Books 2003
1 3 5 7 9 10 8 6 4 2
Copyright © 2003 by Madonna
All rights reserved

Designed by Toshiya Masuda and produced by Callaway Editions, New York
www.callaway.com
The moral right of the author and illustrator has been asserted
Made and printed in Italy
ISBN 0–141–38048–9

Visit Madonna at www.madonna.com

All of Madonna's proceeds will be donated to the Spirituality for Kids Foundation.

MADONNA RITCHIE was born in Bay City, Michigan. She has recorded 16 albums,
and appeared in 18 movies, including *A League of Their Own*. She lives with her
husband, movie director Guy Ritchie, and her two children, Lola and Rocco, in
London and Los Angeles. Her first children's book, *The English Roses*, was released
in more than 100 countries around the world in September 2003.

LOREN LONG lives in Cincinnati, Ohio, with his wife, Tracy, and two sons, Griffith
and Graham. He has taught illustration, and his work has been featured in numerous
publications, including *Sports Illustrated* and *Time* magazine. An avid baseball fan,
he played on a vintage team for many years.

A NOTE ON THE TYPE:

The body text in this book is Hoefler Text, a family of typeface designs which was
originally developed for Apple Computer from 1991 to 1993. The display type is
Hoefler Titling, designed in 1996 to complement the Hoefler Text series. Both faces
were inspired by sources such as Jean Jannon's Garamond No. 3 and Nicholas Kis'
Janson Text 55. All fonts were designed by The Hoefler Type Foundry Inc.